This book belongs to

PaRragon

Bath · New York · Singapore · Hong Kong · Cologne · Delhi · Melbourne

NARRATOR	RICK ZIEFF	
WOODY	TOM HANKS	
JESSIE	JOAN CUSACK	
REX	WALLACE SHAWN	
MR. POTATO HEAD®	DON RICKLES	
BUZZ	TIM ALLEN	
ARMY SERGEANT	R. LEE ERMEY	
ANDY'S MOM	LAURIE METCALF	
ANDY	JOHN MORRIS	
HAMM	JOHN RATZENBERGER	
LOTSO	NED BEATTY	
BONNIE	EMILY HAHN	
MRS. POTATO HEAD®	ESTELLE HARRIS	
ALIENS	JEFFREY PIDGEON	
SLINKY®	BLAKE CLARK	

PRODUCED BY TED KRYCZKO AND JEFF SHERIDAN

EXECUTIVE PRODUCER: BRIAN MALOUF
ADAPTATION BY PUBLISHING GROUP

© DISNEY/PIXAR
℗ 2010 WALT DISNEY RECORDS/PIXAR ANIMATION STUDIOS

This is a Parragon book
This edition published by Parragon in 2010
Parragon
Queen Street House
4 Queen Street
Bath, BA1 1HE, UK

ISBN 978-1-4075-9580-1
Manufactured in China

Andy's heading off to college in a few days. What will happen
to Woody, Buzz and the rest of the toys? To find out, read along
with me in your book. You will know it's time to turn the page
when you hear this sound.

Let's begin now....

Over the years, Andy had a lot of fun playing with his toys. He took his toys with him wherever he went: to Pizza Planet, to birthday parties or to a friend's house for a sleepover. And after a long day of fun and adventure, Andy would fall asleep next to his old pals and dream about all the games they would play the next day.

But like all children, Andy grew up. In a few days he'd be leaving for college. The toys were worried. They hadn't been played with for years, and they were afraid that Andy had forgotten all about them. Quickly, they came up with a plan to get Andy to notice them. They huddled inside Andy's toy box with his cell phone. Jessie held another phone in her hands. Woody looked around at his friends. "All right, guys. We got one shot at this. Everyone ready?"

Jessie nodded. She dialed the cell phone's number, and the toys held their breath as the phone rang. Andy reached into the toy box and pulled the phone from between Rex's tiny arms. But when no one spoke, he hung up and left the room. The toys were devastated.

Rex tried to be upbeat. "He held me! He actually held me!"

But Mr Potato Head knew that playtime was over. "Who we kiddin'? The kid's seventeen years old."

Woody sadly shook his head.

Andy's toys weren't sure what to think. Would they be stored in the attic, never to be played with again? Or even worse, thrown away? Buzz wanted the toys to be prepared. "We're going into 'attic mode', folks. Keep your accessories with you at all times."

But Sarge and the Green Army Men didn't want to wait around. They climbed up onto the windowsill. "War's over, folks. Me and the boys are movin' on." Then, one by one, the soldiers jumped. The other toys watched in horror as the Army Men's parachutes opened, and their friends were carried away on the wind.

Woody tried to calm the other toys down. "No one's getting thrown out, okay? We're all still here. I mean, yeah, we've lost friends along the way... but through every yard sale, every spring cleaning, Andy held on to us. He must care about us or we wouldn't be here."

The toys nodded. They hoped Woody was right. Andy wouldn't let them down. Quietly, they went back to their places.

Buzz walked over to Woody. "Whatever happens, at least we'll all be together."

Later that day, Andy was playing on his laptop when his mum came into the room to help him pack. "Anything you're not taking to college either goes in the attic or it's trash." When she saw all of his old toys, she suggested that he donate them to Sunnyside Daycare.

Andy looked over at the toys. "Mum – no one's gonna want those old toys. They're junk!"

His mum sighed. "Fine. You have till Friday." Then she walked out of the room.

Andy went over to the toy box and lifted the lid. He grabbed a trash bag and began tossing the toys inside. When he got to Woody and Buzz, he paused. There was Woody, his old friend. And Buzz, with his wide grin. He looked back and forth between the two. Finally, he dropped Woody into a box marked COLLEGE. Then he threw Buzz in the trash bag.

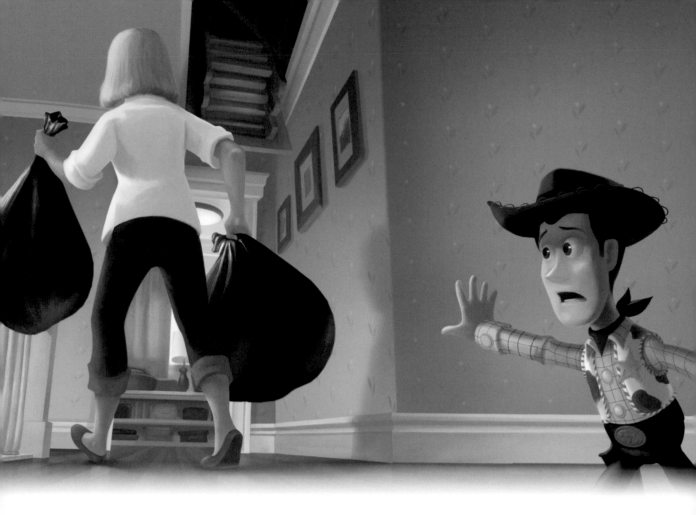

Andy closed the bag and brought it out to the hallway. Woody popped out of the box, shocked. He couldn't believe Andy was about to throw out all of his old toys! Quickly, Woody followed Andy into the hall. He sighed in relief as he watched Andy pull down the ladder to the attic.

But before Andy could bring the bag of toys up, he went to help his sister, Molly. He left the bag on the floor. Andy's mother walked by and picked up the bag. She carried it out to the curb with the rest of the trash. Frantic, Woody ran outside. He had to save his friends!

Inside the bag, the toys were panicking. "We're on the curb!"

Buzz started pulling at the bag, but it wouldn't tear. "There's gotta be a way out!" The toys heard the rumble of the garbage truck approaching. They were running out of time!

Then Buzz noticed something. Rex's pointy tail could cut through the plastic! The toys all pushed the dinosaur against the bag. Finally, it broke open. The toys hid under an empty recycling bin as the garbage truck pulled up to the curb.

Woody made it outside and ran straight for the pile of trash bags. He cut one open and trash spilled out. He tried another one, but still no luck. Then, the garbage man reached for the pile and tossed the bags into the back of the truck. Woody gasped.

Then, a flash of movement in the garage caught Woody's eye. "What the heck?" The toys were climbing into a box in the trunk of the car. Jessie was herding everyone inside.

Buzz hesitated. "Jessie wait. What about Woody?"

"He's fine, Buzz! Andy's taking him to college! Now we need to go!"

Making sure the coast was clear, Woody ran to his friends. "What's going on? Don't you know this box is being donated!"

Rex was hopping with excitement. "We're going to day care!"

Woody tried to explain that Andy had meant for the toys to go to the attic, but no one would listen. Jessie crossed her arms. "Andy's movin' on, Woody! It's time we did the same."

Suddenly, the car door slammed shut. They were on their way. On the ride to Sunnyside Daycare, Woody tried to convince his friends that Andy loved them all.

"He was putting you in the attic!"

"He left us on the curb!"

When the car pulled into the Sunnyside parking lot, the toys saw kids running and laughing. Jessie patted the toy horse in excitement. "We hit the jackpot, Bullseye!"

The toys watched through the box's hand slots as they were carried into one of the classrooms. Hamm looked at the other toys. "So now what do we do?"

Woody sighed. 'We go back to Andy's! Anyone see an exit?"

Mr Potato Head ignored the cowboy. "Exit, shmexit! Let's get played with!"

The box tipped over, spilling out the toys. The day-care toys came over to greet them.

A truck raced across the room and screeched to a halt. A plush pink teddy bear hopped out. "Welcome to Sunnyside, folks! I'm Lots-o'- Huggin' Bear. But please, call me Lotso."

Rex stepped up beside Lotso. "Mr Lotso, do toys here get played with every day?"

Lotso smiled. "All day long. Five days a week."

Lotso showed the new toys around. "You've got a lot to look forward to, folks. The little ones love new toys!" He led the toys into the Caterpillar Room. "Here's where you folks'll be staying."

Then he went back to the room with the older kids. Andy's toys heard the children laughing through the windows.

Rex was growing impatient. "Oh, I wanna get played with!"

Woody had seen enough. "Look, everyone, it's nice here, I admit. But we need to go home."

Buzz walked up to his old friend. "Our mission with Andy's complete, Woody. And what's important now is we stay together."

Woody looked at his old friends sadly. "I gotta go." He walked out of the room, leaving the other toys behind.

Bullseye whinnied as Woody walked away. Buzz tried to comfort him and the other toys. "Woody's going to college with Andy. It's what he's always wanted."

Just then, the bell rang. Footsteps thundered down the hallway toward the Caterpillar Room. Rex ran to the door. "At last! I'm gonna get played with!"

The children shrieked when they saw the new toys. But Andy's toys quickly discovered that day care wasn't the happy place they had imagined. Jessie's hair was dipped in blue paint. Rex's tail was snapped off. A boy put Mr Potato Head's eye in his nose. Hamm was covered with glue and coated with macaroni and glitter.

Meanwhile, Woody had been found by a little girl named
Bonnie. She took the cowboy home to meet her toys – a hedgehog
named Mr Pricklepants, a unicorn named Buttercup and a
triceratops named Trixie. Woody needed their help. "I just need to
know how to get outta here."

Bonnie's toys were very friendly, and they wanted Woody to stay.
They told Woody to relax. Bonnie played with the toys all afternoon.
She held Woody up to her cheek after a pretend ride on a spaceship.

"You saved us, cowboy! You're our hero!"

Woody had forgotten how great it felt to be played with.

At Sunnyside, Andy's toys were tired and upset after a long day of being tossed around. Buzz went to talk to Lotso about having the toys moved to the room with the older kids.

Lotso's gang was gathered in the vending machine, playing a game. They were talking about Andy's toys! An octopus named Stretch said they belonged in a landfill. Buzz had to go warn his friends! Lotso and the other day care toys weren't nice at all.

But suddenly, a large baby doll grabbed him. "Let me go!" Buzz struggled, but it was no use.

Lotso and the others reset Buzz's memory so he would forget everything.

In the Caterpillar Room, Mrs Potato Head realized she had left an eye at Andy's house. She could use that eye to see what was happening there. Andy was packing for college, and he looked very upset. "He's looking for us! Andy's looking for us! I think he did mean to put us in the attic."

Jessie was fired up. "Guys we gotta go home!"

Suddenly, the door to the Caterpillar Room opened. Lotso and his gang wouldn't let the toys leave.

Buzz wasn't any help. He tackled Rex and then herded his old friends into cubbies. "Prisoners disabled, Commander Lotso!"

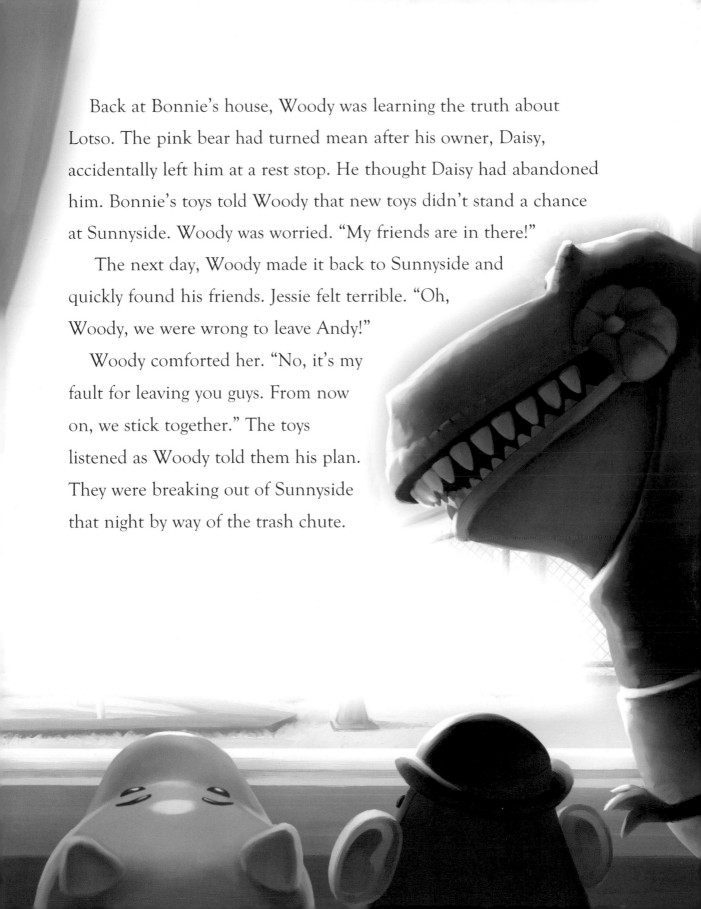

Back at Bonnie's house, Woody was learning the truth about Lotso. The pink bear had turned mean after his owner, Daisy, accidentally left him at a rest stop. He thought Daisy had abandoned him. Bonnie's toys told Woody that new toys didn't stand a chance at Sunnyside. Woody was worried. "My friends are in there!"

The next day, Woody made it back to Sunnyside and quickly found his friends. Jessie felt terrible. "Oh, Woody, we were wrong to leave Andy!"

Woody comforted her. "No, it's my fault for leaving you guys. From now on, we stick together." The toys listened as Woody told them his plan. They were breaking out of Sunnyside that night by way of the trash chute.

That night, the toys worked together to put their plan into action. Hamm and Rex tried to reset Buzz's memory. But Buzz started speaking in Spanish! He was back on their side, though. As quietly as they could, Andy's toys began hurrying across the playground. Woody waved everyone along. "We're almost there!"

The toys made it to the trash chute and everyone climbed inside. Then they had to climb across a pit of garbage to the Dumpster. But Lotso was waiting for them. "What are ya'll doing? Runnin' back to your kid? He don't want you no more!"

Woody was furious. "That's a lie!" Then he told Lotso everything he knew about Daisy. "She loved you, Lotso."

Lotso wouldn't listen to Woody. But Big Baby did. He'd been Daisy's toy, too. And he was angry that Lotso had told him that Daisy didn't love them anymore. Big Baby lifted the bear and threw him into the Dumpster. The toys heard the garbage truck approaching. They had to get off the Dumpster! But before they could, Lotso grabbed Woody. The toys couldn't pull Woody loose. The truck came and lifted the Dumpster. Trash spilled into the back of the truck, and the toys tumbled into the mess. "Ahhh!"

Luckily, everyone was okay. The truck was on its way to the city dump. Along the way, Buzz was jostled back to his old self. When the truck reached the dump, the toys were dropped into a pit of trash.

"Ahhh!"

Suddenly, the toys were pushed along with the trash onto a conveyor belt. They were headed for the shredder!

Jessie noticed a magnetic belt above their heads. The toys all grabbed on to something metallic and were lifted to safety. But the magnet dropped them onto a new belt – one heading for a fire.

Woody motioned to Lotso, who was standing beside the STOP button. "Hit the button! Hurry!" Lotso looked at the button. He smiled. Then he ran away.

The toys were quickly approaching the fire. Jessie turned to Buzz. "Buzz! What do we do?"

The space ranger held out his hand. Jessie grabbed it. The toys all held on to each other as they headed toward the fire,

Suddenly, a shadow loomed over head. A giant metal crane swooped down and plucked the toys out of the trash.

Woody turned to see the Little Green Aliens sitting behind the controls. "The Claw!" They always knew it would help them get home.

ATTIC

The toys were finally safe. They caught a ride on a garbage truck back to Andy's house, then snuck inside. The toys all climbed into a box labelled ATTIC, except for Woody and Buzz.

Woody held out his hand. "This isn't good-bye."

"Slinky Dog popped his head over the side of the box. Have fun at college!"

The other toys all wished Woody well. Buzz just smiled. "You know where to find us, cowboy."

Woody and Buzz each climbed into their boxes. When Woody was all settled in the COLLEGE box, he heard Andy's mum in the hallway. "It's just – I wish I could always be with you."

"You will be, Mum." Suddenly, Woody had an idea. He jumped out of the box and scribbled Bonnie's name and address on a note. He put the note on top of the ATTIC box and then climbed inside with his friends.

When Andy saw the note, he decided it was a good idea to give his toys to someone who would love them. He drove over to Bonnie's house.

Bonnie was playing outside. Andy brought the box over to her. "I have some toys here. These are mine, but I'm going away now, so I need someone really special to play with them."

Andy handed the toys to Bonnie one by one. He was surprised to see Woody. "He's been my pal for as long as I can remember. You think you can take care of him for me?"

Bonnie hugged the cowboy.

Andy and Bonnie played with the toys for a few minutes. Then Andy headed for his car. He looked back to see all his toys beside Bonnie. "Thanks, guys."

Bonnie went inside with her mother as Andy drove away. Woody watched Andy's car get smaller and smaller. "So long, partner."

Buzz sat with his friend. The toys would always love Andy. But now they had a new kid to love, too. And they had each other.

They knew they would be just fine.